Remembering

SIMON & SCHUSTER BOOKS FOR YOUNG READERS • An imprint of Simon & Schuster Children's Publishing Division • 1230 Avenue of the Americas, New York, New York 10020 • Text © 2023 by Xelena González • Illustrations © 2023 by Adriana M. Garcia • Book design by Laurent Linn © 2023 by Simon & Schuster, Inc. • All rights reserved, including the right of reproduction in whole or in part in any form. • SIMON & SCHUSTER BOOKS FOR YOUNG READERS and related marks are trademarks of Simon & Schuster, Inc. • For information about special discounts for bulk purchases, please contact Simon & Schuster Special Sales at 1-866-506-1949 or business@simonandschuster. com. • The Simon & Schuster Speakers Bureau can bring authors to your live event. For more information or to book an event, contact the Simon & Schuster Speakers Bureau at 1-866-248-3049 or visit our website at www.simonspeakers.com. • The text for this book was set in Fertigo Pro. • The illustrations for this book were created using acrylic paint on paper. • Manufactured in China • 0623 SCP • 10 9 8 7 6 5 4 3 2 • Library of Congress Cataloging-in-Publication Data • Names: González, Xelena, author. | Garcia, Adriana M., illustrator. • Title: Remembering / Xelena González ; illustrated by Adriana Garcia. • Description: First edition. | New York : Simon & Schuster Books for Young Readers, [2023] | Audience: Ages 4-8. | Audience: Grades K-1. | Summary: "On Día de los Muertos, a family prepares an ofrenda for their favorite furry family member, remembering all the ways that their beloved pet brought love and comfort to their lives"—Provided by publisher. • Identifiers: LCCN 2022053279 (print) | LCCN 2022053280 (ebook) | ISBN 9781534499638 (hardcover) | ISBN 9781534499645 (ebook) • Subjects: CYAC: All Souls' Day—Fiction. | Pets—Fiction. | LCGFT: Picture books. • Classification: LCC PZ7.1.G6533 Re 2023 (print) | LCC PZ7.1.G6533 (ebook) | DDC [E]—dc23 • LC record available at https://lccn.loc.gov/2022053279
LC ebook record available at https://lccn.loc.gov/2022053280

Remembering

To Marcos,
May you enjoy
your time with
your animal friends.
Love + Light, Xelena González
2023

Written by **Xelena González**

Illustrated by **Adriana M. Garcia**

SIMON & SCHUSTER BOOKS FOR YOUNG READERS

NEW YORK LONDON TORONTO SYDNEY NEW DELHI

To Buju Cat and all the big-little loves who have touched my heart: Querina, ChaCha, Chauncy, YiYa, Guera, Spotty, Xina, Rhett, Paco, and Santo
—X. G.

For Simon Limon—your fierce, fluffy love lives in my heart always!
—A. M. G.

Today I prepare your favorite meal
and serve it in your special place.

I gather all your treasured toys
and bring you the brightest flowers.

I whistle the notes you liked the most,
the ones that mean it's time to walk.

And in the wind I hear your reply,
like an echo in my heart.

The rain joins our rhythm
with a click-clack-tappity-tap.

I dry my tears and pour fresh water for you, my constant companion.

Today I walk our trail alone
to bring more memories home. . . .

A bit of earth and a bright red leaf . . .

a warm stone to skip, and a crooked stick
you would have made your own.

The house seems empty without you here.

So our family fills it with photos and stories
until we feel like you are near.

Together, we light candles and make a path of petals
to guide your way home, on this sacred night . . .

when we welcome back our loving, loyal friends.

This is how we thank you
for your fierce protection
and your warmth on cold nights,

for the comfort you gave on sad days
and the smiles you offered on bright ones.

This is the way
we remember you.

Author's Note

In 2018, Adriana and I had the good fortune of traveling around the country in support of our first book, which allowed our artistic dreams to come true. That same year, life dealt us major heartbreak as we both lost our beloved pet friends. My Buju Cat grew very sick and died after being by my side for seventeen years. Soon after, Adriana's dog, Simon, suffered an illness that took his life after fourteen years of companionship.

We won many awards that year, but we lost our best pet friends. Looking back, we like to think that our little buddies traveled with us for as long as they could and accompanied us into this next phase of our lives, where we would have the courage to become independent artists and to share new stories with the world. Still, we miss Buju and Simon very much, as we have missed our animal friends who have come and gone before them.

I buried Buju in my backyard, and that is where I sat when I wrote the first draft of this story. It was a way to ease my own heart and to offer comfort to my amiga Adriana, who was also in mourning at her own house down the road. In the years since then, I have sent copies of this story to various friends who have expressed grief in losing their own pets. This is a way of showing compassion and a way of remembering.

It is also an invitation to be part of a beautiful tradition passed on from our indigenous ancestors who saw death as an important part of life, like one continuous circle. Día de Muertos has always been my favorite time of year because it helps me remember this important truth and to be less afraid of something that is very natural for us all. It is also a time of revelry, with many colors, joyful memories, and customs, plus lots of good food and music!

Now the spot where I sat and cried for many days is decorated every November with vibrant flowers, a toy mouse, Buju's food dish, and many of the same elements you see pictured in this book. If you feel called to honor your pet in the same way, you may use this book as a guide to help you build your own ofrenda. It is a beautiful and creative way of showing we remember.

—X. G.

Illustrator's Note

My little furry friend Simon was a long-haired black Pomeranian. He came to me when he was three months old because a friend couldn't take care of him. I instantly fell head over heels in love with the little fluffy butt and squealed in joy, "I love you so much!" The very next thought was *It's gonna hurt when you're gone!* Fourteen years later, Simon, that bundle of glam-rock flowing hair who accompanied me everywhere, passed away. No longer would I hear the pitter-patter of paws that I came to expect every morning. It hurt badly. If you have lost a pet, you know the feeling.

It has been healing to work on this book. I'm so glad my friend Xelena shared her poem with me. By painting these pages, I got to honor my dog Simon's memory and the paw print he left on my heart. Creating this artwork also helped me grieve other losses I've experienced. Plus, I think it is special that, within the tradition of Día de Muertos, we take time at least once a year to remember our loved ones in a positive way.

I love to paint people I know and the faces that remind me of home. So for these illustrations, I asked my friends Quiahuitl Alejandro, Isamar, Sebastian, and Quiahuitzin if they would be willing to help me tell this story. They agreed. They, too, had recently lost their pet cat, Indigo. We got to hang out for a day and took pictures of what we thought Xelena's words would look like. I also took pictures of my new furry canine friend, Annie, who is a short-haired black Xoloitzcuintli. These photos helped me create the illustrations for this book. I cut up the pictures and then rearranged them like a puzzle to come up with ideas for the words. I ended up creating twenty paintings using acrylic paint on paper. I hope the artwork speaks to you and helps you grieve any special companions you might be remembering.

We would like to note that some people do not include photos of the living on altars for the dead. In order to visually tell this story, we chose to include pictures of the family with their pet.

—A. M. G.

Building your own ofrenda

BACKGROUND

Every year, after the festivities of Halloween have passed, a new celebration begins throughout Mexico and many other parts of the Americas. Known as Día de Muertos (or Day of the Dead), this tradition usually spans two days, November 1 and 2. Although traditions vary, the first day is often reserved for remembering the angelitos, or inocentes. This refers to children or animal friends, who are considered "little angels" or "innocent ones."

GETTING STARTED

If you'd like to build your own ofrenda, or offering, the main things you'll need are a quiet mind and an open heart. Choose a nice place outdoors or indoors to make your guest feel welcome. Your offering can include favorite foods and drinks, as well as any items they enjoyed in their lifetime. For pets, this may mean toys, blankets, and treats. For humans, these items could include books, music, games, and other hobbies. Displaying their name and photos is a nice touch.

ADDING THE ELEMENTS

Since this custom has strong ties to indigenous culture, many ofrendas have symbols of nature's elements: earth, water, fire, and air. Can you find all four elements in the story?

Earth can be represented by rocks, wood, sand, seeds, or anything that grows. Water might be poured into a glass for a human or into a dish for a pet. Fire and air are usually offered through candles and copal incense. Please make sure an adult handles the fire for you.

Finally, the cempasúchil flower (or Mexican marigold) adds bright, golden colors to the mix. You can even create a path of petals, leading from outdoors to indoors.

MAKE IT YOUR OWN

Just as our pets are each unique, our offerings to them will also be one of a kind. Different families build ofrendas in different ways, with dates and customs changing according to region or tradition. Some people may even add a mirror to their ofrenda, as a reminder that life and death are part of one continuous circle.

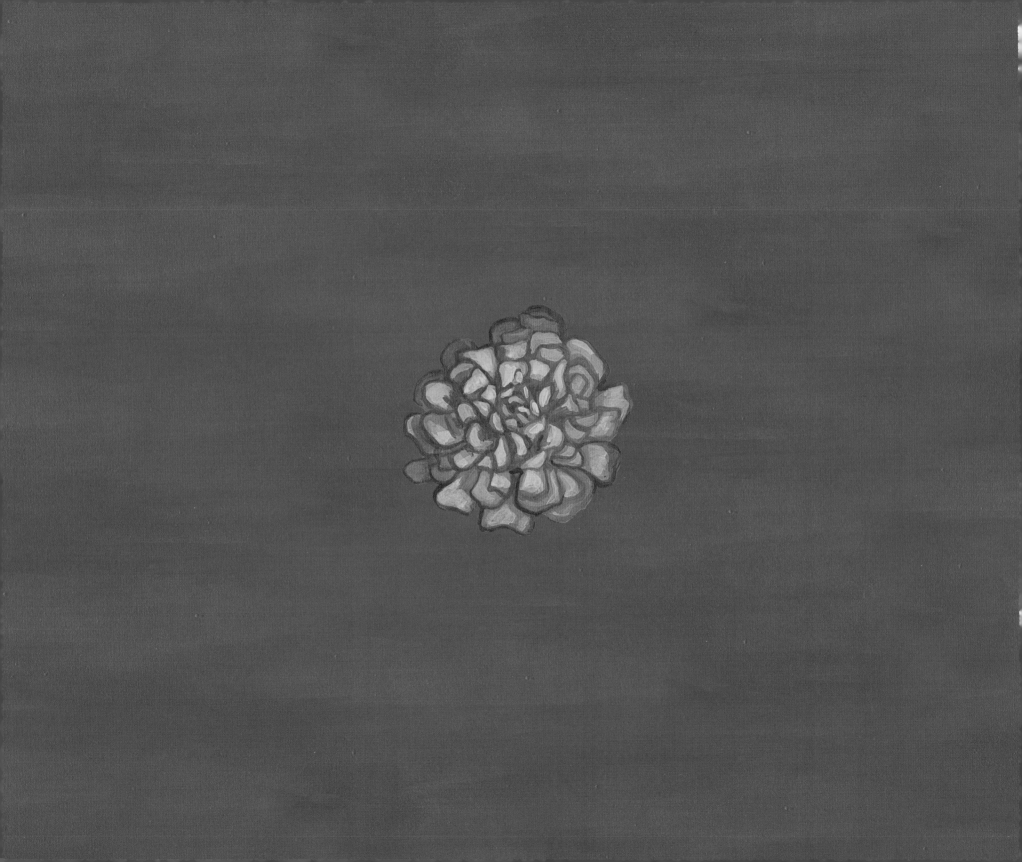